For Mrs. Gaston, my 10th grade English teacher

ISBN: 979-8-9918351-0-7

Publisher: Laura Austin

Chapters:

Chapter 1

In the Beginning

In the beginning, the earth was without form, and God was hovering over the waters. When God saw all he had created, he knew it was good. But when the world had become corrupt, the people of the world looked for their own way to create a utopia. They believed the solution to creating a utopia was pure, innocent happiness forever. The only way to achieve this pure, pristine glee was to edit the human DNA to remove unwanted emotions. The problem was when you edit DNA, there is always a chance that a few people will still develop emotions. David Stevenson was one of these people, born into a hospital on the eastern side of the Great Island. Inside the hospital, it was cold and dark, with white walls, tiled ceilings, and gray floors. His whole family was there to view David's birth, but like most toddlers, David never cried, whined, or complained. He was such an extremely obedient and self-controlled child that his parents, Bob and Linda, never could tell if David had other emotions because he acted just like they did. As time progressed, David had thoughts that brought feelings, but David didn't know what would happen to him if he had an outburst, and he figured he was supposed to act like his parents.

At the age of four, when David started school, his mother stumpily walked him into the school building where on the floor he saw brown carpet. David also noticed that the walls and ceilings were white as his mother continued walking. She stopped in front of room 219 and read the nameplate, "Mrs. Carnival."

The teacher, Mrs. Carnival, was all fun and no work. She led the class through an introduction while bouncing around the classroom like some kind of wacko. Another person knocked at the door, and Mrs. Carnival walked over and opened it. The children saw hundreds of games of Monopoly on a cart. She told the person,

"Thank you Stephen,"

grabbed a few of the games, and Stephen entered. She shut the door gently, like a sloth setting down a branch, and set the games out on everyone's table. One of the classmates, Gordon, started reading the rules aloud, so Mrs. Carnival went along with it and applauded him for his courtesy. David was so competitive he went straight for Boardwalk, rolling the dice over and over again. David was losing the entire game and starting to get angry, but as he was about to flip the gameboard over, the lunch bell rang.

At lunch, David went through the food line waiting to get his apple and burger. He saw a poster with the food pyramid, and he noticed the wall's color was tan. He handed the lunch lady his five dollars as she said,

"Have a nice day."

During his meal, David sat with a large group of nine people, and when he asked if anyone wanted to be friends, they would agree, but they wouldn't talk to him. David loathed 12:30 PM—right after the meal and recess, Mrs. Carnival would show short videos about stories like "The Tortoise and the Hare" and other famous tales; during this time she would watch the kids talking but never try to stop them; she was content with it. David, on the other hand, hated the chatter. David looked around the room and saw kids drooling with it dripping out of their mouths, other children banging on the desks, hand sanitizer being thrown about the room, and loud screaming every few seconds, yet no one seemed to care except for David.

Later, at around 1:30 PM, Mrs. Carnival presented quartz to the whole class to excite the children; To David this was stupid, and he mumbled to himself,

"It's quartz, it's all over my yard at home. Why do I need to see this?"

David finally stopped to look around at the classroom with plastic posters on the wall showing the ABCs with animals, a gray counter in the back of the classroom for children to get hand sanitizer if needed, and cabinets above that counter; there were four sets of desks, each with three to five students at them. A marker board and Promethean board could be found on opposite walls in the room. Mrs. Carnival made a seating chart at 2:00 PM, and she told the class, "I thought I'd make a seating chart tomorrow, but it was more convenient to make it today." Seating charts were still customary to make, but it was more a part of the culture than a method to keep control of the classroom. David was forced into the seat next to the door, where he would have to get up every ten minutes for the kids that couldn't help using the restroom every hour.

This was his first day of school, and as time was nearing 3:00 PM, the class prepared to leave. David hadn't truly made any new friends, for he was afraid of standing out; he still wanted friends but didn't want to be good friends with anyone. David knew being recognized as different from the group could mean catastrophe for him. When it was 2:58 PM, Mrs. Carnival, who had been trained to catch the "freaks out of line," stared him down; he rotated around, feeling stress in his ribs, and glared at Mrs. Carnival. Since it was normal behavior, he smiled, and she looked away as the bell rang. Mrs. Carnival finally told everyone,

"IF you are a car rider, go outside the front of the school,   IF

you are a bus rider, go to the back; IF you have YMCA, go

to the cafeteria; I release you."

- - - - -

David walked out to the car rider line; looking at every sign on the walls, and he came across one that read, "BE GREAT." Once he had eventually arrived, he looked out the double glass doors; Mr. Pierce came around and yelled

"LEWIS!"

Thinking back, David remembered that during the school day, Lewis was one of the kids in his class. A few minutes later, Mr. Pierce came in and shouted,

"DAVID!"

and he walked outside to his mother's red sedan. On the car ride home, his mother asked him,

"So, how was the school day David?"

His hesitant response made Linda puzzled. Hesitating wasn't something people did, but she thought, *maybe he isn't that bright.* David proceeded to tell his mother, "Mrs. Carnival was so much fun; everyone came up to talk to me, and we watched a short film about the tortoise and the hare, along with a lot of other ones." For the rest of the car ride, David watched the trees go by in the car window and read the building titles as they passed, "Dr. Lays Dentistry, Two Way Diner, Fun Town, Pizza Pantastic." Upon arriving home, David ran inside, sliding open the glass front door, and went through the yellow-walled living room and out the side door. His friends, he found, were animals instead of people, for dogs were like him: happy, angry, sad, and fearful. George and Silver, (the dogs), were fun although David thought it fun to mess with the dogs and make them mad because it was the only other place he could find these expressions. He would often throw the tennis ball, but with their laziness, David was getting the ball more than the dogs. When he came back inside, he considered watching TV, but with a Big Purple Dinosaur, which might haunt him in his dreams running across the screen, he quickly turned it off. After hearing

"I-M-A-G-I-N-A-T-I-O-N"

spelled out on every channel, which was how it always was, except for the news, that was only about murder, David got up off the blue sofa and moved to turn on the outdated dark brown ceiling fan, because it was 90 outside. He began to smell food cooking in the hallway behind him. With sweat dripping off his forehead, he thought, *Ahhhh Chicken.*

He went to the kitchen and asked his mother,

"When will dinner be ready?" She happily replied,

"Around 20 minutes or so; you can go run outside, play with the dogs, or go to your room; although I don't know why you would, there's nothing to do in there."

David decided to go into his room and wait in the dark. While waiting, he daydreamed, thinking of a

Peach-Tree that could walk; it walked around, with peaches that would fall off for the people to take, but when night came, it would stuff its feet in the ground and obtain nutrients to grow new fruit for the next day. One month, though, no rain came and the soil dried up. The walking Peach-Tree struggled through the small town and found no one wanted its dried fruit. As the Peach-Tree grew weaker, the people became more unpleasant with the Tree, but the Tree continued offering food, so the people cut its branches. The Tree walked back to its usual planting area for the night and found that the once fertile ground had become so dry it couldn't put its legs into the dirt and couldn't use its branches to help for support. The poor Tree chose to run for a week at a very slow pace; eventually, though, it happened to find other trees like itself and decided to live with them. David heard something and looked around quickly at his bed, desk, and the paintings he had on his wall. Paintings of cows, ducks, and other birds, as his mother yelled,

"DINNER!"

for the second time.

David opened the solid oak door to his room, walked down the long hallway, and sat down at his chair in front of the large, maple wood table to eat the chicken, corn, and green beans his mother had prepared. Bob arrived home, and

"HEY HONEY,"

are the words he got out as he opened the door and also proceeded to sit down at the table. The family was quiet as they scarfed down all the food they could eat.

Everyone was heading down the hallway to bed when a noise of shattering glass came from the front door. Bob and Linda continued through the hallway unphased, but when they saw a man wearing an all-brown suit run in, looking around and yelling

"LIBERATION! LIBERATION!"

David saw a burst of excitement on Bob's face when he was shot straight through the head. With blood exploding out of his head like a hose, Bob happily uttered his last word,

"YAHOO!"

Collapsing on the ground, David shook fearfully, grabbed a pair of scissors from his desk and threw them at the maniac as his father gently fell on the floor dead. Although the scissors did nothing, the wacko conversed with Linda telling her, "I'm goin through the town and killin one man in every home." David looked around and saw that everyone was happy except him, and even he couldn't express the signs of exerting a teardrop from his eyes. The man exited the room at that moment, but David wanted vengeance. He couldn't though, for his enemy would be happy to die. David had to keep a straight face since it didn't mean unhappiness to most people, and David knew this, so he kept his expression flat until he ran to his room and wept. Linda called pickup services for the body the next morning at 6 a.m. When the assistance arrived, she paid them 90 dollars, and Bob was gone, but the blood stain was never removed from the light brown carpet. At 7:30 Linda woke David up and told him,

"You need to get ready for school."

As much as David would have liked to complain and tell her no, he didn't want to say no to her at this time. He stared at the trees as they passed, avoiding every building interrupting his view. Once they arrived at the school, David walked up the steps to the front glass door of the large brick structure. The day before he had thought it was an odd place since it lacked sidewalks, unlike most other public property. David continued to his classroom, stepped in, and curved his face to a fake smile. Only today was different—when David sat down, he heard a sound behind him, "Psss pssssss psss." David turned around and saw a kid making strange noises. This kid was bullied yet liked the attention. David thought maybe he was trying to bully him, but when he didn't, the kid gently spoke,

"My name is Clay, and yours is David right?"

David considered not saying anything, but responded with,

"Yes."

The school day progressed as usual except that at lunch Clay would talk to him about what they did for fun and everything, but David still had to express artificial joy despite being deeply distressed by his father's death. They both sat at the same table alone, unlike the previous day when he had sat with a large group. After the school day when David was walking outside, he read a poster on the wall that proclaimed, "Death is Freedom." David thought nothing of the poster as he continued with his everyday life.

He continued in a loop of going to school five days out of the week, usually talking to Clay throughout the day, and after lunch watching a video during which the teacher, Mrs. Carnival, would often give him an odd stare. She frequently took the children outside for an extended recess that could go for hours, and the kids could run around playing tag happily, but Clay and David would always stand off in the distance watching the children play tag, oblivious to everything in the world. Although an extended recess was against school policy, they wouldn't fire a teacher for a basic infraction such as that. School no longer was a house of learning, and it became more obvious to David as the year went on.

Eventually, the time came for Christmas break. The Christmas party was on the last day of school before winter break, and it was David's job to bring the cookies, yet he forgot them at home, so when he finally arrived, David was disappointed in himself. No one else even noticed that he had forgotten the chocolate chip cookies except for the teacher, Mrs. Carnival, who had a checklist, but it was fine by her.

Mrs. Carnival brought out the board games and indicated that,

> "If you want to go outside and play on the playground, you can, or you can play the board games I have or just rest."

Mrs. Carnival went outside with the majority of the children since some of the parents were inside who could watch the few who stayed in the classroom. Clay noticed that David had stayed inside and offered to play checkers with him, and he agreed. Clay would laugh when he lost and laugh went he won, and although their understanding of the game was equal, David still found it tormenting. Even worse, his father, Bob, had taught him how to play checkers; after a few games, they decided to eat some of the food provided and began consuming Cheetos, Doritos, cupcakes, and Oreos, all laid out on black tables outside Mrs. Carnival's room. When it came time to leave at noon, the teacher told everyone to pick up the mess they had made, yet none of the students cared; they were too busy talking to each other about their home lives, how delicious the food was, and how they'd wrecked each other in the game of tag. The Cheetos, Oreos, and cupcakes had been thrown everywhere.

Mrs. Carnival exited the school building with the students and parents, only going so far as to turn off the light to the classroom as she looked backward at all the other eleven classrooms in the hallway and went to her black mini-van. David walked outside; looking for his mother's sedan, he sat there waiting and waiting, but she didn't arrive until another two hours had passed, and by that time he was bored, and his legs had grown stiff from sitting still for so long; David acted excited that she was there as he hopped up, kicking pebbles from the ground up into the car through the door. David asked his mother,

"Why were you so late?"

His mother explained that she was extremely late because she thought the school had only made the school day an hour shorter, and she had been tired from working a fifteen-hour shift at the Big Mart supermarket the day before.

On the car ride home, David's mother, Linda, was speeding, traveling forty miles per hour over the speed limit, which was already fifty-five miles per hour. David peered over at his mother, and she was falling asleep behind the wheel, so he shook her, and she awoke to find herself swerving left and right on the road, hitting small bumps and cracks until the car ran off the road and into an enormous tree where Linda went flying out of the busted-out window since she didn't have a seat belt on. She badly injured her right leg. David was one of the few people who still wore the seat belt instead of viewing it as something optional, but the few lose threads keeping it together didn't hold, and he went flying upward and forward into the glass windshield, cracking it. David nearly passed out as his mother called 911. Linda lay in the grass on the edge of the forest with her leg up against the tree they had hit. The ambulance was slow to arrive, although Linda maintained a thrilled attitude; When they finally arrived, they conversed with each other,

> "No one has called an ambulance in over a month now, let us see who we have here."

They took David and Linda to the hospital, and the siren hurt David's ears the whole time, but he kept his eyes closed. The EMTs pulled him out on the stretcher, but he didn't quite understand since he hadn't necessarily been seriously injured. He'd only hit his head. He could feel the people gradually strolling up to the doctor, and after using anesthesia, the surgery commenced on the back of his head. It had been five years, and offices had been switched around, and, surprisingly, David ended up in the very same room in which he was born.

Chapter 2

Into the darkness

David opened his eyes after two and a half hours to find the world had turned black and white; David knew this meant he was colorblind, but when he looked down at his lime green tee-shirt, he could still see green; his blue jeans were still blue. David still had hope until the doctor touched him and the color of his skin instantly became visible. David realized that anything he touched he could see the color of it, but he saw the world in black and white. He tested this theory, holding a penny from his pocket, it looked its usual copper color until he dropped it, and it immediately changed to a dark-gray. David ran down the long, white hallway past the double doors, up the stairs, and into the restroom; he looked into the mirror and saw the gray walls behind him and the dark gray stall doors. Then David came to himself and saw gray tones. After walking back and watching the clean floor in disappointment, David noticed his mother's running shoes and proceeded to look up at her with a phony cheerfulness that hid the truth behind his eyes. David was glad that his mother's leg seemed completely healed although she still had a subtle limp. The doctor had asked Linda,

"Would you like to pay now or wait until you get home and get a bill?"

She had very little money remaining, so she said,

"I will wait to get a bill in the mail," and the doctor replied, "okay, if you would like to leave now, you may."

So David and his mother left, calling a tow truck to bring back the car that somehow still worked perfectly. They went to the grocery store and drove into the parking lot. David noticed many of the spots were being taken by two cars parked sideways and trucks in the middle of the yellow lines. There was only one empty parking spot, but when Linda was about to drive into it, another car took it before she could. They parked their car in the lane outside the car, trapping it, and David pushed the door open and hopped out, looking up at the brown paint on the building that read Big Mart. Linda and David walked onto the concrete path and trudged in through the automatic glass doors; after arriving inside, most shelves were half empty, and David saw a plastic divider where they obtained a shopping cart. As David went around the Big Mart with his mother, there were large posters that read, "Only two allowed of each item," but his mother was grabbing five and placing them in the cart's basket, so David asked,

"Mom, can we afford this?"

and she responded,

"Of course, we have plenty of money."

David looked in the basket and noticed it was piling up and thought, *With this much food, how could she be lying*. He looked up at the big steel shelves containing fruit his mother grabbed. Linda walked around to the frozen area at the back of the store, where it was a complete mess, and she struggled to find chicken legs and broccoli. The corn and peas she found on aisle twenty-two, which was on the opposite side of the store. As they trekked along, David asked his mother,

"What color is the floor?"

and she gazed at him with a noticeable delay before telling him, "it's light blue-green." David looked down at the tiled floor in sadness. David perked up quickly, though, as he lifted his head and asked for lard with the food because it made all of it taste so good. Linda agreed since it was only one aisle over at twenty-one, and noodles were located on that row. When it came time to pay for the food, though, Linda strode past the pay counters at the front of the store. The cashiers were holding scanners in their hands waiting for anyone to come by and pay for their food. David was surprised, but no one stopped to ask, "Are you going to pay for that?" as they continued outside. Once arriving back at their car, they found the front had been busted open from being hit and further dented. The BMW in front was no longer there. When David's mother tried to close the hood of the car, it wouldn't, so she resumed putting the groceries into the back of the sedan. She asked David, "Can you go put the shopping cart into one of those cart holders over there?" He obeyed despite carts being littered throughout the area, even on top of some trucks and minivans.

When David started walking back to the car, he watched a man get out of his car and move around perfectly fine despite being in a disabled parking place; He also observed that the man lacked a permit to park there, but Linda stepped out for a second and told David to hurry up, so he ran and jumped in the sedan with his mother as she was preparing to drive off. David and his mother lived over twenty-five minutes away from the Big Mart, so since Linda didn't want to talk to him, David figured he would continue his previous daydream.

The Peach-Tree had found other peach trees, but when morning came, the hot sun rose above the horizon, and the Peach-Tree found that the other trees couldn't walk around and were trapped in the ground; at first it thought, *Maybe they only have stuck their feet too far into the ground and can't get out. I Must Help Them!* but his branches were still quite short. The weak Tree could not pull them up, so it resorted to asking if they needed any help and got no response; the other trees were not so life-like as itself. The Peach-Tree was frustrated by the other trees, and it yelled,

"Have you no dignity to wake up in the morning, you wretched trees."

In the following months no people came for the Peach-Tree, but its branches grew longer, and it thought, *I can now pull the other trees out of the ground; they'll see what the world is like after all, won't they?* When the Peach-Tree struggled to pull its first tree out of the ground, it waited for it to loosen and thought, *Whoa! no wonder they never went anywhere, they're really stuck in the ground here.* Finally, after much excruciating effort, the tree fell out on the ground and found that the peach tree lacked the legs to walk but had roots sticking out of it instead. Once the Peach-Tree saw this, it was frightened. *Are they all like this?* it thought.

The Peach-Tree, confused, ran to an isolated hill past the field of peach trees and saw a man coming up the opposite side of the hill. The man pointed at the Peach-Tree, and it ran, but it was too slow, so the man caught up with it quickly, grabbing the Tree. He took the Peach-Tree to his house and told it, "Stay here, I am going to bring some of your old friends." Dazed, the Tree decided to stay where it was and waited as the man returned with two other men. The Peach-Tree saw they were holding knives as they got closer. The Tree recognized the two people, for they had helped cut off his branches before. At once, the tree began trying to run, but it couldn't because the man's giant hands were around it as he cut off its legs and planted the Peach-Tree in the ground. The man then told the Tree,

> "I'm sorry, but we don't want a peach tree running around. We only wanted a tree that produces peaches every day."

In the coming days, the Peach-Tree felt roots coming out of its stem. Steadily, its roots grew longer, the peaches came out slower, and its ability to speak and think became weaker, but as the Tree watched the people, it understood the greed of the three men and was angry. It couldn't do anything as it wished it could vow revenge.

The Peach-Tree's vow of revenge did not last, for a day after the vow, it lost its ability to think forever and was nothing more than an ordinary Peach-Tree. As an ordinary Peach-Tree that no longer produces peaches, the three men found no use in it anymore and chopped it down for firewood. Inside the wood, only mere memories remained, and as the three men threw it into the fireplace, it became like a furnace, and the house went up in a blaze. The three men died along with the ashes of the Peach-Tree. The house was destroyed with nothing left standing as the Peach-Tree's ashes blew out into the wind in the morning light. The three men's judgment had come in the end.

David woke up the next day in the car after having fallen asleep in the sedan. David's mother came in and informed him that Christmas was only a day away. He considered getting his mother a present as it was something his parents had always done for him. David strained himself to devise a good gift for his mother and finally decided to make a piece of art. This was the first time David had used a computer since Windows slowly loaded up on their ancient computer. David had seen the Chrome app, and in school, they had been shown computer mice. He figured, *How hard could it be?* as he hovered the cursor over the chrome's bright, multicolored logo and double-clicked. David proceeded to the search bar with the white cursor and saw it change to a different symbol. He discerned at first glance that it was some kind of, "I" and googled, "zebra," gradually moving the mouse with his tiny hands over to the bar that read, "images." David struggled to click the mouse. After finally getting to the zebra images, he looked at hundreds of pictures until finally deciding on the first one. David walked over to grab the paper he needed from a gray cabinet behind the computer desk where he sat. David then walked back to the computer and sat at the large, rolling, wooden chair for a second time as he opened a drawer and got a pencil to draw it. David was about to start drawing, but perceived that the image was too small. He thought about it for a while as he moved the black mouse over the image and clicked on it, expecting something to go terribly wrong, but it got significantly bigger like he wanted.

David could now commence drawing as he produced what he thought was an amazing work of art, adding red, blue, purple. *Ah, my masterpiece* David thought as the black and white zebra exploded off the page. In his heart, David believed it was his masterpiece. The next day, David got up early only to find nothing set up for Christmas; His mother was usually up extra early on special occasions, so he woke Linda up and told her, but she seemed unaffected. David was confused why she couldn't steal like she did with the food at the supermarket, as he thought back in his memory to the other day. David remembered there were Christmas gifts on aisle four, but they were kept locked up at all times unless someone brought the money for them and Linda didn't.

David still gave his mother the gift, and as she looked at the art piece,

she told David, "Thank you."

Despite her response, David was disheartened since he was expecting an ecstatic reaction but only received content feedback as he watched her put it into a drawer in the kitchen. David, for the first time in his life, considered running away as everything he ever did for his mother received only mediocre praise. When David thought about it, though, he quickly dropped the idea as his mother was still useful for food and shelter, until one day she seemed to speak differently, so David asked,

"Are you ok mother?"

and she replied in a very gentle, slow manner,

"I think I may be ill; do you want to come with me to the doctor?"

David did, so he nodded. On their way, though, they stopped at the red gas station, or a gas to-go, as it was called, to get a drink. She told David to fill up the car with gas. She felt very thirsty, and rushing in to get water, she searched through the refrigerated section with seven different groups of drinks, and the last section on the edge contained water bottles. She grabbed one, ran out and jumped in the car yelling,

"GET IN THE CAR DAVID,"

so he put the gas cap back on and plopped himself inside. David's mother yelling at him got him excited at first because her tone of voice sounded angry, but when David was back in the car, he discovered she only wanted to get there faster and didn't want to have to open the car door to inform David, so she yelled.

Once arriving at the doctor's, she ran inside from the front of the hospital, which only contained eight parking spaces. Linda then asked the front desk,

"When can the doctor see me?" The woman told her,

"In forty seconds."

Linda looked around the room at the three, black fold-out chairs in terrible condition which were put out for the people to sit on. David and Linda then sat down on the two chairs, but as they snapped beneath them, they both fell on the mildly wet carpet floor. The room shook as a mammoth of a doctor wandered out of his yellow-painted office. Conveniently, there was a meter stick for measuring glued to the wall for children, and David used it to estimate the giant's height as six-foot-ten inches. The doctor laughed his big laugh as he looked at David and Linda with their backsides wet. The doctor made it clear to them that the office did that on purpose, to liven up the room since patients were rare. It was funny to have them drop on the floor. As they went into his office, David noticed another poster on the wall in the waiting room that contained a graph showing the different potential levels of happiness from one to seven, with a color code that went from red to green, although the red and red-green was crossed out. As there were no negative emotions, and if one did have other emotions, they were an accident brought by nature. The doctor proceeded to ask Linda,

"Have you had symptoms of anything recently?"

and she told the doctor,

>"No, I've just been really thirsty and tired lately."

David's mother then stated to the doctor that,

>"My husband died recently, but that shouldn't really change anything."

The doctor laughed, at the thought of someone telling him a husband dying would make one tired and thirsty, and he mentioned to Linda,

>"My name is Dr. Gary. I probably should have told you that earlier, if you didn't see the sign above the door that says it already. Anyway, if you want me to do some tests I can, but I've seen this many times. It comes and goes for many people."

Linda did still want to do the tests, so she asked the doctor,

>"Well, when can you do the tests?"

and the doctor responded,

> "come back tomorrow. Our instruments are old, so we have to make sure they still work and make sure to clean them."

So the next day, Linda and David returned, and the woman at the front desk acknowledged them and led them to the back. The doctor did a lot of testing, with big machines and small ones that looked like dinosaurs about to bite into them. Neither David nor his mother had ever seen these machines before, and she had to lie down to go through them. Dr. Gary later told her,

> "Your results look very good; you are expected to live for another ten years."

Linda then looked at him and asked,

> "Why do I have only ten years, though?"

Dr. Gary sat down at his desk and declared,

> "The god of the government in all his love has brought you a sickness Cancer."

Linda gazed at the doctor, satisfied with all he had said, and she was pleased with having Cancer, but David was not. David was the one who asked,

"Is there any treatment for Cancer?" and the doctor answered,

"Ha right!

Your son is funny.

There hasn't been a treatment for Cancer in over a hundred years."

David considered this for a moment and realized this meant that he would have to take care of his mother for the last few years of her life, and that whole time she would be completely happy to die. David then wondered what the backstory was as to how the people came to be this way, and he pondered long and hard on a question for which he would never know the answer to. In the distant past, while messing around with human DNA, the people who brought about the Utopia including the famous Dr.

Mikhal, figured that having everyone cheerful and happy was the best idea. After achieving that success, there was no point in going any further into gene modification. Their were simple, they rounded everyone up and gave them a pill that edited their DNA. The scientists, who brought it about, took the pill also and were happy with anything that came or went, and the people with Cancer or other illnesses would be happy in the face of any situation or problem that came their way. Dr. Mikhal thought that he had made it so that other emotions wouldn't happen along ever again, but he was wrong and had to deal with a few people who did know what the other side was like. Dr. Mikhal was later given a job working for the police force, and he was called, "The Happy Doctor." Since he was always happy, why would he not enjoy the attention he recieved for being called "the happy doctor"? Dr. Mikhal later found that removing other emotions helped bring shy people out of their shells. Shy people were no longer afraid to speak up, and people with mental illness were either no longer bullied or wanted to be bullied more. Unity as a whole came to society under Mikhal; the world as a whole no longer cared about deadlines, extreme working conditions, or deadly events that happened to them.

Chapter 3

The Others

David continued living life as many years flew by and he joined middle school. On the Great Island, this was the year of school that having eight teachers throughout the day was normal. He never learned the teachers' names in school as they never told the students what their names were. The parents knew only what classrooms their children were supposed to go to, not the teacher or subject. Clay was somehow in four of his classes, so that was who he had to talk to throughout the days as they passed.

When September came, the school implemented a new policy of monthly medical checks. The first students to go informed the others how it was and what would happen with taking a multi-question test on many random subjects being common during the medical check. David would go to class, and it seemed empty since he ignored the words of every teacher because it wouldn't affect his life whether or not he listened-except for on the day of the check. Teachers were not expected to turn in students who acted out of place; It was rare, and no one knew the true reason for the monthly checkups. The classroom walls were a bright white, and when the school nurse opened the door to take Clay, she smiled,

"I'm looking for Clay,"

she told the teacher, and he got up with cheerful glee and walked out with her, closing the light brown door behind him. The reflective walls shone on his face; Clay was hiding something—David could tell. He waited, zoned out in the classroom, and the nurse returned as Clay entered.

"May I ask for David to come now,"

and he went as she smiled a more wretched smile. They walked down the hallway together through a long corridor with green and white tiles on the walls. Large double doors stood there and were opened.

"Alright now, David, you can sit down," announced the nurse.

The nurse walked hastily over to her desk and looked through the filing cabinet as David sat down. The happiness she portrayed was weaker than others despite her miserable smile, but as she opened the folder, her joy increased greatly as she began prancing around like a panther chasing its food, and he wondered what had made her so happy. The principal stepped in through the double glass doors they had previously entered,

"Hey David,"

uttered the principal as though they had met before, wearing his usual black suit and tie he often wore in the hallway. There was a hint of evil happiness in one of his eyes that seemed almost cruel, and he questioned David, talking almost too quickly to be understandable as if wanting him to slip up.

"Have you ever noticed Clay out of line? Do you have any other friends or only talk to him?

Would you ever think of him using other emotions? Would you think of yourself as having many emotions?"

David was surprised but knew the correct responses to the questions, bearing in mind many of the students truly believed they had other emotions-as a different state of happiness-until they were told otherwise. If one's response was,

"of course,"

it was usually a dead giveaway they didn't have other emotions, but they asked the rest of the questions to make sure. He had considered responding yet stayed quiet, staring at the dark-brown wooden desk in front of him, pretending to be happy and stupid as ever. Although the principal knew he was faking the stupidity, he couldn't determine anything else and released David back to his class. He watched Clay a bit more after that and wondered why his monthly check was so different from the other students and how Clay was involved.

The next day Clay appeared to have been beaten; there were marks all across the side of his face, and when he asked about what happened, Clay would speak in a tone indecipherable from sadness or happiness,

"Oh nothing, I only tripped,"

and the injury on his mouth would open as he talked. It was almost like his friend had other emotions like him, an-other of some sort. At first, David was excited but was quickly reminded by the blood sliding down the left side of his face that this wasn't as great as he previously thought and that there still was the chance the injuries and pain only made him appear to be sad even though he wasn't sad at all. David stared at him,

"I know your secret; you have other emotions don't you?"

Whispering, Clay responded,

"What do you mean? There's sadness and happiness. What else is there?"

The shock was shown on both of their faces like masks coming off as they pondered what to do now, but for Clay, the shock manifested itself in sadness.

Their attitudes toward each other changed; although Clay knew full well David was the reason he had been beaten; David noticed that he didn't seem to immediately rebuke him as a friend, and he thought it was odd that Clay wasn't angry at him, despite their friendship. This had been a turn in their friendship as Clay had only two emotions. Gradually, Clay and David stayed further and further apart from each other until they only talked once every few days. The only reason to split apart was realizing they had other emotions, neither wanted to be turned in since Clay didn't want more sadness to come, and David was fearful of what would happen if he was turned in.

Around a month later, Linda didn't show up to the school to pick him up, and David sat there waiting after school for a few hours until he figured he would have to walk home. After arriving home, Linda was on her bed and had forgotten to pick him up because she noticed a lump on the side of her body. David knew it was his mother's cancer growing. However, the lump didn't worry her since she physically couldn't, but it was enough for her to forget about picking David up from school.

David worried about his mother; though, but she didn't notice. The rains poured, and with each day his mother came fewer and fewer times to school to pick him up as if their mother-son kind of friendship was dwindling because of this sickness that had come upon her. The rains came month after month, and David sat in the school building alone during the rains, for it was impossible to see through. The school was practically invisible to him since the steel ports for students to walk under were the only things he could see. It would have been too risky to go straight through the rain; he would be guaranteed to be hit by a car. One day out of every twenty there was no rain. David walked home through the neighborhoods behind the school to his house and watched the trees and the rundown homes as they appeared very dirty and were all white with ages-old paint and broken windows. Once David arrived home, though, he would only ask his mother for lunch money, and he would eat dinner there with her, never saying a single word. The school turned off the lights after six o'clock, meaning David would have to wait and sit alone in the darkness all night with no end to the rain in sight. Then the next day would come, and instead of his mother driving him in her damaged red sedan with a completely warped front that would be hard to believe functioned, David sat at the school observing the rains filling themselves a never-ending glass of water. The teachers enjoyed the rain and the darkness that came with it as did everyone else, even Clay, who no longer talked to him. David didn't have any human interaction until one day he began to think more strongly about running away, which he had always considered, but never actually took action to fulfill his plans.

He decided to talk to Clay about this idea since their chances of getting caught were slim because no one cared where they went or what they did, but Clay didn't respond the way he had expected, telling him,

> "I don't want to run away; it isn't worth it. Here we have food and shelter; why would I want to give that up?"

It came as a surprise to David, who thought *for sure he'd want to go and leave to the outer edges of the island where we could live away from what has become of human kind.* The problem was Clay was pleased with everything he had, and he didn't see anything wrong with society like David did. This meant that David gave up the idea of running away because he would be alone with nothing to do but live off what the wilderness provided him for food.

Gradually, the days between the great rains grew shorter, yet the flooding was great, and cars became hard to drive on the streets in the low parts of the island where it was flooded. With some houses completely underwater, many people drowned in their houses since they didn't care to leave their homes or die in their cars. They drove straight into high water areas without a care in the world of what would happen to them as their cars filled up with water causing their deaths. David would usually avoid these parts of the Great Island as he didn't want to find all the dead people in that area. Government agencies were assigned to clean them up, but those groups were usually slow. Since the workers would be happy whether they cleaned up the bodies or not.

David started going home again, but instead of eating his mother's homemade dinner, he would ask her for money, and after she gave it to him, he would go eat his favorite food at a place called The Pizza Corral, which eventually became where he always ate dinner. Despite chowing down his favorite food(cheese pizza), he never felt fulfilled by it. He was stuck in an unsatisfying, boring life. Whether he was walking home or at school, he would have to keep living with his mother until he eventually could move out.

One day David woke up and found he was late for school. He wondered why his mother wasn't up yet. He went and checked in her room, and she was still sleeping. He figured she wouldn't go anywhere, so David took her car keys and started out the door. David knew the drive was only about ten minutes, so he thought it would be easy, but since he had never driven a car, it took around thirty minutes as traveling at a faster speed was stressful to him. At least parking wasn't a hassle. No one cared if he parked in the middle of the road or on the sidewalk. When David entered the school, he found that many of the students were missing, and as lunch came, he walked into the lunch line as usual holding onto the steel bar and looking at the moderately-gray floor which normally would be a golden brown color.

The lunch lady didn't have much food to provide, only a small piece of oddly dark green broccoli with more stem than top, and some soup in a small cup that looked like throw-up, but since David was hungry, he decided to eat it anyway as he went to his table. It was disgusting. He could feel his taste buds mourning for the food of the past. The food he wanted was no more, and upon driving home, nothing was to be found in the fridge to eat or drink; it was empty shelves. David held his hands over the sink, and he was glad to find the faucet could still put out clean water to drink.

Linda walked in through the unpainted, wooden hallway to the kitchen.

"I will make you dinner in an hour or two; do what you will for now."

In his head, he was questioning how she would manage to make dinner without any food.

So David went outside to play happily with his dogs and mess around with them, rolling around in the grass and having fun. The dogs were his companions, his last friends, and no one would take that away from him. George and Silver were getting old, though, and it was likely they'd die in a few years. David would throw a red ball across the yard, and George would always get to it first, so every once in a while David would pretend to throw the ball and then throw it a few feet for Silver to go get and bring him back to him.

After a few hours, David came inside and looked at his mother, who was sitting around, not making dinner. The maple wood table had plates on it, so confusion was in his mind. David headed to his room through the oak wood door and waited, moving his mouse around on his computer without actually turning it on. He then decided to grab a book on the desk to read. He was curious it didn't have a title on it, but he quickly got bored when he discovered it was an autobiography he had forgotten about on the life of Dr. Mikhal that he had put there a few months earlier.

David decided to get up and go check what his mother was doing, and when he arrived in the kitchen, he fell on the floor. He saw the massive wounds his mother had inflicted using a kitchen knife to stab George, with blood from his dog dripping on the ground. David wanted to stab Linda badly and knew full well he would never get in trouble for it, and she would be perfectly happy if he did so, but David didn't go through with it; after all, his dog was some of the only food left available.

Linda cooked the dog in a frying pan on the stove as David waited patiently at the table, and although he was sad about the death of George, Silver was still outside for him to have, as cut-up meat and organs would last them a while. David was unusually calm when Linda brought out the dog meat on a normal white plate, and he ate slowly and quickly spit it out and re-ate his food despite its bitter taste. David no longer let Silver out of his sight; he had to make sure his mother didn't cook him. So David kept the dog in his room or kept Silver on a leash from then on, watching Mother closely.

As the month passed, David kept checking the fridge's plates of dog meat—a slice here, a slice there, it didn't seem to be going away any time soon, until there was about half left, and he knew it was growing in importance to watch out for Silver.

"We should eat tree bark and grass Mom,"

informed David. She wouldn't mind eating Silver, since eating bitterly disgusting foods may displease David, but it wouldn't be unsatisfactory for her.

Linda got the idea to make soup, so she filled her large steel pot with water and added a bit of meat and some blades of grass. When she got around to pouring it into David's soup bowl, he slowly put the brass spoon to his mouth. Finding it better than expected, David willingly slurped his soup down, expecting that his dog would potentially live another year. Later, his mother moved most of the meat into the freezer as it was no longer going to disappear quite so quickly with hundreds of bowls of soup able to be made out of the meat.

With a year's worth of food, David was satisfied; he didn't need to watch his dog to the extreme anymore, apart from keeping it away from other people. For that year, more food was shipped to the island, and more food was successfully grown there, so by the end of the year, there was no danger of Silver getting eaten, and life returned to normal when the waters receded and the ponds that had formed evaporated.

David's mother was walking slower, and her slight limp was no longer slight. The next few years came, and his mother wasn't walking at all anymore, so he would bring food to her. Driving himself to high school, David was tired of being alone, he wanted to meet someone, not caring whether they were going to be happy forever. In his determination, he looked around in the high school all day, looking after classes in the long hallways, for people he thought he might want to be friends with, but there was no one, and when he came home, his mother was so weak she could barely walk, so David made sure she ate more than usual for dinner.

Linda kept getting weaker and weaker until David decided he would take her to the doctor again; even though they weren't close anymore, David still cared enough to not want her to die, although she'd gleefully walk into a pit of magma. On the drive over, David continually looked over at his mother to see if she was okay. The trees outside were a dark gray, but to his mother they were a bright green, and on the way, the area around the roads was very forested. He drove up to park, but when David turned once more to see if his mother was alright, he noticed the large bump on her side. He quickly looked at her face, only to notice that she wasn't breathing. Linda was dead, and the doctor's office was closed.

Chapter 4

Life

David went to high school the next day, thinking of how alone he would be—taking care of Silver, as his dog would be the last creature that he could call his friend. David walked around with his dog on a leash everywhere from then on, which mostly meant home and high school. At school, David was frustrated and alone. He wanted to quit going to high school, and he very well could, but where else could he meet people?

One day in his classroom, he saw a young woman on the opposite side of the classroom and wanted to go over and talk to her, but he was afraid to go. He gradually got up from his desk and walked over. He asked,

"Would you like to go on a date?" she stared happily at him before saying;

"Yes,"

she would have probably been willing to go out with anyone, though.

On the night of this event, David was worried she wouldn't show up at the Eatery of Garden, but after about fifteen minutes of waiting, she finally arrived. The waiter came and sat them at the booth in the farthest corner of the store to the right of the restrooms.

"What would you like to drink?" asked the waiter.

"I would like some water," stated David,

and his new friend wanted tea. When looking around, no one was there except for the waiter who was currently getting their drinks. The menu had several items crossed off of it, so the only thing available was chicken with carrots and soup, so that is what they each were going to have to order, but when the waiter came back, he brought the food with him, already knowing what was available on the menu. They sat there eating lunch as David questioned her,

"So how is your family?" and,

"Good, good,"

she would reply in every circumstance. The date was about to end as they were finishing up their food, so David mentioned,

"Maybe we could do this again sometime, like next Tuesday," and she responded quickly,

"Yes."

This pattern continued for a few years until they had turned eighteen and were about to graduate high school. David began to want something more out of this relationship; he went to the diamond store, looking around at racks of clothes and glass at the front of the shop selling the rings, and when he saw the largest diamond ring, David reached out and grabbed it from behind the counter. It was easy to walk out with, mainly because the employees didn't care if anyone stole stuff; they only worked there to play games with everyone else. David decided to wait until after graduation to give it to her, though, and this week he wanted to ask her if she wanted to go do something other than eat out. She came over to David's house, and they watched a movie that David thought was very boring, but she thought it was one of the best movies on earth. It was supposed to be funny, but that didn't necessarily mean it would be. A dog was brutally attacked by a bowling ball, which is not what David would ever want to watch.

David was waiting for school to end so he could be out in his life with his dog and friend. The anticipation of this final month seemed to take centuries, so he decided to take up painting and tennis. He found painting to be great. He had to set up so much plastic sheeting over everything, that time seemed to pass like a fly escaping sudden death from one's hand. He was painting: bats, bees, trees, fleas, and peas all over his giant white canvases that he had stolen from the art store. The public tennis courts were always full of people, so David would use his racket and hit the ball against the walls of rooms and buildings as he went through the city. He particularly liked the museum portion of the city with The Museum of Unusual Arts having a big wall on one side that he often used for tennis. One of the days David went inside the Museum, and it had many famous paintings with invented animals and art styles he had never seen before.

David became particularly interested in this form of art and chose to try it out on his canvases, so he ran home holding his racket and tennis ball while observing the concrete he was running on. He noticed his house again anew with its windows and driveway and wanted to make an animal out of it because it might look interesting. So he began to work and enjoyed adding legs and a nose to his newly created animal, and windows for eyes. After about five hours of working, he felt accomplished even though he was only about halfway done, so he decided to skip school the next day to work on his art. David would often go outside and touch parts of his home, like the wood on the outside walls, to see what color they were—what was particularly great about his painting was that he could touch it and see it come to life with bright colors of blue, red, and yellow. He had reached the point where he could tell what colors things were by looking at them in grayscale, but when painting, the final product and the development was still more fun when he could see its color at the end of the day. The driveway became the tongue on his house, and then he added the completing touch, which was David entering the house through the tongue of his newly created animal. David thought it was funny as it brought new meaning to the words "house pet."

The time had finally come for David to go to school and graduate. David arrived at his high school dressed in a cap and gown, and he walked to the football field, up the stairs, and into the bleachers where he could sit down as all the other people came since David was ten minutes early. When the time came for the event to start, the principal walked up and started calling people's names, and David assumed the principal was making a game out of it as he tried to call all the names as fast as possible. David walked up the touchdown line after most of the people had been called and took his diploma from the principal.

David, while waiting for his friend to go and get her diploma, heard the principal call her name,

"Hurry, hurry, come on, come on,"

the principal announced as she was walking away from the touchdown line with the Island Iguanas team name on it.

"Would you like me to drive you home?"

called David in the distance.

As he stood there in the parking lot, she got in his car, and David drove her to his home. He ran inside and came out holding a small black box, and as David grabbed the ring and held it out to her, David saw the beauty in its golden light and light-blue diamond. She looked down at the ring and then stared at David for a moment thinking of how all their time spent together had come to this one minute on the concrete driveway of David's house. She affirmed what David thought by simply handing the word out of her mouth,

"Yes,"

and since culturally this was meant to be the most heavenly moment of one's life, she found great joy in this event. David might not have won her emotionally, but he had certainly won her mind; they decided having a small marriage was best–after all there wasn't exactly much family for David. They went to the "Marry You Now" church and achieved all of her dreams.

David had other ideas in mind—children, and he didn't have much to worry about as she wouldn't care. They went together in the damaged red sedan to their house, and as night fell, in a year, a child rose out of the sunlight. David was happier than ever thinking about how much harder children must have been to raise before Dr. Mikhal changed everything, and for once, David was grateful for what he had done. The sun rose a few more times as David had four boys and a single girl. His life was good, and he was so occupied, he almost forgot he couldn't see the color of the world around him, often watching kids play in the crib or with Silver.

As another year came and went, that pleasure that he once felt began to wane. David didn't find fun in watching his kids run around anymore. Everything His wife did annoyed him at night and constantly invaded his personal space. David began wanting to test his children to see if any of them had his genes for other emotions. He held up Jerry and pinched the three-year-old to see if Jerry would cry, but David found only laughing coming from his son's face. David tested this process with the other children and acquired the same result. This made him think back to how he was as a baby, and David knew he had faked the status quo, so he thought maybe, just maybe, these children were only covering their true feelings. A pinch wasn't going to be strong enough to reveal if his children were fakers, but David didn't want to hurt his kids. He came up with an idea and ran into the kitchen opening the plastic drawers of the fridge; In a small box labeled only as "salted," his hand reached in for a stick of butter. David went over to his cabinet and grabbed a bowl to place the butter in, then put it in the microwave and pressed three, zero, start, and waited for the butter to become oil. This scheme was brilliant, and David walked slowly, holding his bowl, into the children's bedroom and picked up the girl, Martha, pouring butter on her face. Sticky slimy butter-the single most annoying thing in the universe-didn't even twitch a muscle of her face that would hint at discomfort. David duplicated the system with his other boys: Jimmy, Jerry, and Boe, and once again, the outcome was the same. None of

David's children had his genes for deeper emotional understanding, and this gave him a choice. David could stay at this home and have more children, hoping that maybe one kid in the future might be like him, or he could run away somewhere and live alone with no one around but himself to talk to, and he would most likely struggle to survive all by himself-unless there was someone else there with him to go through the whole situation.

Chapter 5

The Cave

David went to go find Clay, as if they both fled to the outskirts of the Island, then they could survive. David wandered around the city looking over the black streets, the tall wooden and steel buildings, and the few cars lining the sides of the streets. He eventually walked into a newly built grocery store; believing that in a city with a population of a million it must be impossible to find people, David walked down aisle six, grabbing broccoli. Then he continued to the frozen section, where some chicken and beef was available at the end where the plastic overhead and plastic dividers between the different compartments containing the food that companies produced. Remembering to get cheese, he went to the left, looking at each compartment, seeing pepperonis and mozzarella in a giant, clear plastic bag, cheddar in a small block wrapped in wax, and cake, until he came to sliced provolone, which he grabbed and continued walking, holding all his groceries in his hands instead of grabbing a bronze cart.

When walking by the onions in their large wooden bins alongside avocados and bell peppers, David saw Clay in the distance about to go out of the store through the large automatic glass doors. David put his groceries down on a table with banana written on the sides of it, but which failed to have any bananas on it since the employees in the back restocked whenever they were told to do so, and the manager in charge of telling them to restock only told them to do so at the end of the week and could be seen playing video games in his manager's quarters. David ran on the gray carpet to catch up to Clay, calling out,

"Clay, hold on,"

only to find it was someone with similar facial features and height;

"My name is not Clay," uttered the man.

David dragged his feet in disappointment, going through the parking lot, searching for his car as the temporary excitement made David forget about the location of the sedan. He remembered the groceries he still needed. David went back in through the automatic doors to grab his food and walk out. He flung the sedan's red, dented, sliding door open to put his food in and after opening the driver's side door, he hopped in and was taken aback from Clay's presence in the passenger's seat. There was a moment of silence then, "I saw that you had been lookin' for me the other day, so I've been following you. I waited for you to find someone that looked similar to me or to ask someone if they knew who I was, and now that has happened." David considered what Clay had said before asking, "Well, I was wondering if you would like to go to the edges of the island where few people live, considering it would be much easier to survive with two people, and I'm sure you want to leave here.

"No, I'm happy to live here, as long as I am never given in to the authorities,"

Clay responded.

"Uh, but,"

David replied before recollecting that Clay knew no fear, he simply didn't want sadness.

"I can give you a recommendation on where to go, if you'd want me to tell you,"

spoke Clay, and David nodded,

"yea?"

"Go straight west from where you live on that road that goes straight, I believe it's 24th street, and once that street ends, keep going; eventually you will run into a large Cave that appears to be all boarded up, but since it is in the side of a large hill, much of it is above ground, and if you knock on the boards ten times, a person will call 'Hello,' to you. You should reply, "Goodbye," instead of hello, and then they should let you in."

At that point Clay took a glance at David to make sure he got all the information he needed and leaped out of the car with his hand on the handle before letting go to run away. David drove home watching the gray trees go by and the yellow stripes become white as he turned the corner to go to his house. David entered through the front door and went through the hallway to his bedroom. He got in bed, laying there for hours until night time came, and his wife got in bed. David thought it was strange how his wife didn't ask why he was already in bed, but she assumed David felt like sleeping, so he got in bed.

The next morning David went to the restroom and looked in the mirror that went up to the top of his head and whispered to himself,

"You will leave today; you will leave today; you will leave today," trying to convince himself into going through with abandoning his family, knowing they would still be happy without him around and would be able to obtain food. The restroom had a woven laundry basket that stood four feet tall and a bronze sink that had turned green from use and because he never used chemicals to remove the green. The faucet was made out of stainless steel. The room was small and the toilet tiny. David left the restroom and sprang over his queen-sized bed with a dark blue sheet and comforter on top of it over to the closet. The closet contained a suit and tie and some t-shirts and shorts hanging up. It was dark inside of the closet. Some of his wife's clothes were on the opposite side, and on the floor in the far corner was David's suitcase, and he reached down to grab it when his wife turned on the light. She asked,

"What are you doing?"

"Oh, oh I was going to throw away this suitcase. I mean, we never go on vacation, so why should we have it?"

responded David.

"Good, I can put some of my stuff there,"

his wife smiled. David also moved the muscles around his mouth upward to give the grabbing his suitcase situation a more normal feel.

David made sure his wife saw him throw the case in the trash as she passed by before swiftly grabbing it back out, brushing off the sticky plastic from the case and rushing back to the bedroom and into the bathroom. David shut the restroom door and locked it before snatching his toothbrush and some toothpaste and casting them into his suitcase. He also seized some clothing from his dresser, which had light-brown wood and knobs to pull on. he took three shirts and some blue jeans, along with some of the shorts from his closet, considering most of the year it would be slightly warm in the cave and hot outside, the jeans would only be for winter. He threw in five pairs of underwear too.

David thought about taking the car, but he didn't want to take too much away from his family. David went into the garage to find a bike since the cave might be far, so walking was a bad idea. He grasped the bike in his hands before going to the brown-red shelves touching it to see its color and to obtain tape. David took his suitcase and put it on the front of the bike. Then using the tape, he wrapped it around the case over and over until he got tired of the duct tape sticking to his hands, so he wouldn't have to hold his suitcase. The bike, he discovered to be red. After bouncing on top, David rode out of the garage, pressed the remote he had taken out of the car to close it, and went on his way to the Cave.

The sidewalks frustrated David as he'd often have to get off his bike and get back on when ordinary citizens walked by. The road appeared to go on forever as it went into the horizon line. After three hours the street lines stopped, but the pavement kept on, and this gave David hope to continue onward since the road might end soon. The buildings on the side of the street changed–they were not wood anymore, but brick all the way around–a deep red brick that appeared as dark gray to him with a steel roof. He passed a prison, and most of that was wooden fencing that was still in a usual criss-cross pattern of normal steel fences. The main building itself was made up of a lot of glass outside walls and steel inside walls. While David was riding by, he saw a criminal through the wooden fence who had a mentally insane face with a giant nose and a mustache. He spit through the fence at David, and the criminal died while laughing. David stopped and put his feet on the ground then dismounted from his red bicycle, and he glared at the dead prisoner who was very thin, and despite it being very easy to escape a wooden fence, the prison had been inactive for many years, and the criminal had been kept in. He saw the criminal, and in a strange way it reminded David of his mother. This wasn't out of place to David, who, without flinching, mounted his bicycle once again and continued for the Cave. Another twenty minutes passed before David could finally see the edge of the road in the distance, where there was a dead-end in between two adobe buildings. David's thoughts discouraged him: *How do I know this Cave is even safe? What if these people turn each other in? Why did Clay say they boarded up the Cave?*. The Cave apparently wasn't so easy to find with rolling hills and small rocks covering the terrain. One would find it difficult to ride over with a bike. Bump, bump he heard struggling along and pushing hard on the black pedal. He examined the hills for a wooden area covering when "click," his bike caught a rock, and David went flying off onto a pointy boulder. After Checking the bike, David found that it was alright; then he inspected his arms, and observed that a massive open wound was on his arm. He noticed it when the searing pain came. He got on his bike, hoping that the people at the Cave would have bandages to prevent infection and help with healing. The sun's heat beat down, causing his arm to torment him as it started throbbing, and David shrieked before looking up to see the Cave ahead.

He wanted to be excited but couldn't find the necessary energy and didn't want to risk moving his arm. He walked slowly up the hill because running could be a hazard. Grass coated the hill in a bright green which contrasted the moldy dirt-covered planks up the side, and the hill moved inward a few feet where the boards were, which didn't allow enough sunlight for grass to grow, which created a black patch of dirt. The top of the hill didn't seem like it should have still been standing if there was a cave with such weak soil covering it.

David banged on the boards ten times—as he was informed to do—a

"Hello"

was said through the boards so he continued,

"goodbye,"

and a door was flung open that seemed to be old beat up boards, so he walked over to where it was opened. Going inside, David saw that the structure was held up by large concrete beams and a curved several-inch-thick layer of plastic going over them which after touching it, he saw it had been painted a yellow color. The area where the Cave went deeper was blocked off with a wooden board painted yellow to fit in with the rest of the room. The people inside were short and looked half-healthy with poor posture, like someone who pulled an all-nighter to study for a college exam the next day. They saw his wound and chattered,

"We have no bandages for that, but we have towels."

David looked down at his wound;

"I will take a towel,"

he uttered. He had expected more from these people. There were about twenty people inspecting him and checking to see if he was like them. They pinched the unwounded arm,

"Ouch!"

David would babble. Then they pulled out a knife, and he backed into a corner and felt a weakness in his stomach. When the group saw he was mostly like them except for having a better developed sense of emotion than they did; they generated satisfied frowns. The floor was vinyl around the edges of the room and a large square in the center was a rug. David noted this in his mind. He left through the door to go obtain his bike. Walking down the hill he perceived the towel in his hand had many holes and was torn in some places. As he wrapped the dark-blue towel around his arm, bringing terrible agony for a few moments, the threads attacked his bleeding open wound.

He stepped up the hill, taking his bike with him, and pulled on the area where the boards making the door were. The people guessed he went back outside to bring something indoors. He realized that they all had very small vocabularies and often could only understand very basic words. Out of,

"Where can I leave this?"

They only understood, "Where I this," and as they stared in confusion at him, David pointed at the bike, and the group finally understood what he was asking. The people pointed at the yellow board covering the part where the Cave went deeper. "How old were you before you came here?" David asked one of the people, trying to keep his question as simple as possible. The man responded briefly, "Four," also looking into the air as if recalling a distant past never to return. The others quickly joined in relaying the information David wanted. The man he asked was the youngest person to come,

"Eight, twelve, ten, nine, thirteen, nine, twelve, ten, six,"

they seemed to recite as if they did this when any new people came, though they all appeared to be over twenty years old. He went to the area where the Cave went deeper and pushed the board hard and forward before realizing there were twenty small wheels being squashed under the weight of the board that allowed for it to be pushed into a slot that had been built for it made out of a yellow, strong, tinted glass that was hard to see when he was standing off with the other people. He saw that there were a number of bags of food that were sealed, and past that the ground became harder to step on with large rocks. Fridges and freezers lined the walls, which made David feel squeezed since there was less room to move around. There was no obvious way the fridges gained electricity, and when he followed the plugs that went into the wall, there wasn't any apparent outlet for them to go into. He turned his bike around and rolled it in between two of the fridges that all had the letters "FFF" written on them where David observed the text written underneath the FFF "Fridges For Fair." David, after pondering why the company name was phrased weird, supposed the company left price off the end because this was the name that worked better. Once again he stepped over the many rocks and saw some clear quartz in the ceiling; he thought, *I should probably get out of here, air pressure changes the lower I go.*

David thought, *I might teach these people how to speak and convey their ideas*, but he had never taught anyone and knew they would find difficulties in learning new words with such a simple understanding of language. When David came back up to the top of the Cave, he found that six people had been watching him from behind the piles of sealed and packaged food and bread. He saw that close to the surface, where the entrance to the Cave in the hill was, there was some red, hard clay that he could easily acquire and use. He took it and wrote words on the yellow plastic walls, and the group watched curiously. He drew pictures of words, messily with his left hand, for objects they might not know "pencil" was one and "fish" was another, acting out the concept if they didn't understand. David found when drawing a frog on the wall that hard, red clay isn't the best tool for it as the lines are all too thick, and it doesn't look like the animal he imagined, and he didn't think it looked anything like it should; it really only appeared to be a blob.

David discerned from watching the group as they watched him that they didn't quite have all their emotions— similar to Clay. They didn't have a sense of frustration, anger, or disgust, so he became the odd one compared to the rest of them. He left through the door to a lake he had seen in between three hills, which they all also used to obtain water. He cleaned his towel of the blood, now flowing in the lake, and he saw that his arm was mostly healed. After putting his arm in the water, he found a giant scar in the wound's place. He made sure the towel was still wet so he could also clean the floor within the hill and squeezed some of the water out only to make it less heavy. Trekking back over the hills, he found that after a while they were like mountains. After climbing five, David knocked once more on the boards ten times, and since they already knew who it was, one of the men opened the door and let him in and surveyed the outside, looking around suspiciously at all the rocks, hills, and crevices, and David noticed that one of the twenty wasn't there. David threw his towel on the floor to clean it and worked hard pushing it across the floor with it scrunched longways so it could cover more surface area. He pushed up and down and to the side, although after the first time of bringing the towel down, it was covered in dirt. He thought about putting all the dirt into a pile and then taking it outside. He used his towel to carry some of the gunk from the floor to the door and tossed it out. The people who saw this weren't grateful and didn't even care about how dirty their living space was; they were happy with the extreme level of dirt, which would have disgusted and frustrated anyone like David. The next day, a woman in the group, who usually would have gone to get water, told him,

"Why don't you go get the water today?"

So he got the two pitchers that usually were filled with water and left for the lake. At the lake, he took one pitcher and scooped into the lake, after that, David took the other pitcher and did the same. When he was around four hundred meters away from the Cave, he saw six people he had never seen before on their way to the boards and front door with masks on and a large can on their backs with a tube that came to their hands. David watched, falling to the ground before starting to crawl closer. A number of trees on some of the hills blocked the people's view of him. He saw them knock ten times, and the group inside opened the door, and by the time the man was trying to close the door, it was too late. The gas from their cans flew at the man, and he gasped for breath.

He held his hands out at the six people before slowly, gently falling and smashing onto the dirt with his face flat in it, his final breath blowing at them. The people opened the door and sprayed into the group. They split up and ran around the room hoping to get away, but they simply had no chance as they gasped for air. The six people never gave them a chance to swing their arms in defense. David could do nothing but watch in horror with only a small distance being a barrier to his own death as they carried the dead group off. He drew near, hoping to get a better look at the people who did this treacherous thing, but because of their masks, he couldn't determine what their faces looked like. He sat in the grass only forty yards away. Then one of them turned his gaze toward David who sat motionless. The guy saw David and quickly called to his partners and pointed at David, who was now running as fast as he could to get away.

Chapter 6

The Wilderness

David ran over grass and massive boulders going through the forest that was filled with many tall, green trees. He dashed in between them, looking back every once in a while in fear. He quickly crossed a small stream, and the dirt was covered in leaves. Then He turned his gaze far into the distance, beginning to slow down. He recalled that his bike was still in the Cave; it was gone unless he went back one day, which most likely would never happen. *My best option for now is to get some sleep since the sun is setting*, thought David; *I've never quite seen one like this before.* It set with many clouds above a few distantly separated trees a thousand feet into the distance and twenty small clouds losing their beauty as the sun faded into the earth.

The morning came, and as the sun rose high in the air, David noticed that all the clouds were gone. He sat there for hours on end trying to think of something to do. *I know I can find some long sticks to build a shelter and to make a fire*, he thought. He could see the forest across the plains he was standing on since it was only a few thousand feet away, and he walked gradually over to it. There didn't appear to be many sticks on the ground, so David got the idea to break some off of the green trees. He bent a relatively large branch; "snap" it went, which became frustrating after a period of time because of how bendy the branches were. He was twisting and turning the branches, and he believed the branches would never come off. David gave up on twisting them and scanned the dirt intently for a rock. His eyes moved to a piece of flint lying against a tree not far from him, and he strided over to pick it up. Holding the brown, chipped rock that was a space-like black, he chucked it at a tree as hard as his arms could throw, and when that wasn't effective,

David went searching into the woods for a boulder. Looking through all the gray oak trees that became gray-brown to the touch, he saw one after a minute or two, so he began running through the thick underbrush before chunking his rock at the boulder, gaining a few flint shards. He must have spent an hour scraping his flint pieces along the giant stone till they became sharp enough to cut tree branches. He walked back at a slow pace but had a feeling that while in the forest, his every moment was being monitored—like there was someone else there, and he thought, *running now will only make it seem like I know*. Once he got out of the woods, he no longer felt a sense of being watched as he could more easily see through the underbrush full of bushes and small plants.

He went back to work twisting the branches of the oak trees that stuck out quite and far then cutting the rest of the branch after it snapped. David continued this process of cutting off branches that were about three inches in diameter, going over some of the bushes and grass to get to them before going around to collect the tree limbs. He cut around twenty and carried five of them off to where he was located, making two other trips through the grass to obtain the rest. From David's perception, the time was about noon. In an expert-like manner, he shaped the limbs into a basic outline of a structure, with the four thickest branches being planted into the ground; then he went out into the plains, collecting long strands of the grass that he could use to tie the tree branch box together. He knew it would be many days before his new house was complete. His stomach began to growl like a pack of wolves about to catch their prey, but there wasn't anything to eat. David took a moment and recalled that in the past Bison had been brought over as food to eat, and every once in a while some would escape out into the wild. He could at least dream of having the chance to catch one of these animals to eat as it would provide food for at least three months if he caught an adult, and a calf would provide one month.

David took one of his sticks and used his sharpened flint to slowly snap, then cut, the end off. He also used his flint to scrape off thin shreds of some of his sticks. He went searching for water, traveling towards the plains, and considering how far he had gone, it only made sense that the ocean was near to where the grasslands ended. He trekked through the grass, his stomach still informing him of his hunger, and in the distance after traveling two miles, he could tell the ocean was only about a mile off and could see its waves far away. David stopped to breathe the salty air into his lungs as he continued on his way. He saw the sand and walked up to the ocean, with his feet sinking. Within a little ways, he could feel the moving in and out of the waves and the crash of the small waves onto his legs, so he held his hands together in the water and rushed over to stand over the dirt and cast it down on the ground before digging a bit further down to find there was some clay. He repeated this a few more times till there was a large amount of smooth wet clay and mud, which he collected and stuck the gunk on the end of his tree limb before sticking his sharp flint piece into the clay-mud mixture. He then tied the flint to the tree limb, which was now a spear, using the long shreds of the limb from earlier. He added more of the clay-mud on top of that and wrapped the outside of the mud in some more of the shreds to help hold the clay there. He took his newly-created spear back to his shelter, and he hoped there was an animal he could catch to eat and a stream with some water that he could drink; otherwise, David would most certainly die. *The city is too far away to go back to* he thought.

The day dragged on as it became the hottest part of the daytime, and David's thirst grew. He was miserable and dehydrated. Instead of going all the way back to his shelter, he began looking for something to collect water in, searching all over the vast empty grasses, but there was nothing. An idea and a memory brewed of a stream he had seen, and David recollected that there was a stream in the forest he had run by, but it was so far away. *I'll be dead when I get there,* he thought. After a period of time, the sun was setting once again as David lay in his frame of a shelter, trying to figure out what to do —*I suppose I'll wait for nightfall and then go get water; it will be cooler then*, he thought. He picked himself up off the ground, and with his spear in hand, went traveling through the woods. He went slowly over every large root that stuck far out of the soil and around the bushes too tall to step over. Sometimes his head scraped the tree's sticks and branches that stuck out to where his neck was, and he would forget to push them out of the way or try and go under them, and the tree would get him, which was very annoying, and if the branches were large enough, they could knock David onto the dirt. He looked around in sudden confusion,

"Uhh uh where am I?"

he stuttered;

"hehehello, is someone there?"

There was a tall person wearing a brown-gray suit and green hat far-off across the stream, and David knew the color of his hat by how often he had seen that color in both gray-scale and normal color.

"He's after me,"

David said. He Appeared to have his face covered with a gray-brown mask. He held his spear in hand, ready to throw. As he drew near his face, he cast his spear at the man, and the man was hit. David could see his light-tan shirt (light-gray) above the spear with the man's chest covered in a thick-red blood (dark-gray). David rushed to the stream to take a drink of water, and he fell in and drank. He didn't know if it was a good idea to drink a lot of water all at one time, so he decided to take one ten-minute break after drinking all that he wanted, but he drank in a slow manner. He looked around for the man, but the man was somehow gone, and the man must have put his spear into a tree as there was a large amount of sap coming out of the gray-brown tree.

After the ten minutes ended, David drank more for the long way back and went on his way--back through the forest looking for animals he could eat on the way. There was a squirrel, and David walked cautiously around the tree it was in. He threw his spear at the squirrel, and it practically jumped into it. He quickly picked up the poor dead animal, and feeling many broken bones, he continued back to his shelter. Some of the wood was dried, so he grabbed some of the grass from the very bottom and pulled out many of the roots with his hands, which turned black with dirt as he created an empty circle of soil. He broke off parts of a large tree limb and scraped off shreds. He then took the tree limb and rotated it back and forth very quickly on the shreds, every few minutes giving it some air and then gently placing the grass over the shreds. Then he rotated it faster than he had earlier, and smoke started coming off of it that David could smell. He was confused as to why the fire wasn't starting, so he took one deep breath in sorrow and blew all over the grass, and fire appeared. In his shock, he quickly grabbed the tree limb he was using earlier and snapped it into many more manageable pieces to throw on the fire before all the grass and shreds burnt up. David stuck the squirrel with a stick he had covered in dirt—to prevent it from burning—-and held the squirrel over the fire, turning it every once in a while to help it cook evenly. He cut it open to help the insides cook. He then took the squirrel, cut its head off, and tried to take many of the bones out, although it was hard. All the hair had fallen out from being cooked, so he held the squirrel to his mouth and took a bite out, chewing for a long time before eating another few bites until the squirrel was gone.

David had taken most of the grass he had pulled out of the ground earlier and placed it in the spot where he would put a bed—at least for now, so he laid down and went to sleep. The next morning, he went to the ocean where there was clay to collect, and upon arrival pushed much of the topsoil off to where there was some very clean clay. He grabbed it and began molding it into a bowl shape. Then he took the grass and made sure that it too was clean of any dirt, then lined the sides of the bowl and a little around the edges, being very careful not to leave any areas where clay was still visible.

David walked back, still holding the bowl from the side without grass on it, then he put it atop a few of his sticks that he had rolled out flat to prevent dirt from getting on it. While the clay was drying, he went to gather more sticks and tree limbs so he could build a wood box to keep meat and food in. He cut many limbs down after his mile-long walk, going back and forth, gradually, putting it together in between trips until he could throw some grass inside and stick it in the sides. Then he put his bowl over the fire to harden it. After three hours, David figured the bowl was done and went to fill it up with mud. Upon returning, he stuck mud in the crevices of his box. This being completed meant he could go hunting for a Bison, and considering there were really only two areas of the grassland he hadn't been to, Bison had to be in both of them as they weren't a rare occurrence and were herding animals. On a monstrous boulder in the distance, there was a single Bison, and David believed there must be a herd over the hill, so he crept to the side of the boulder, hiding from the beast, and when it turned around, he got up and lobbed his spear at the animal. Before it could turn around, David dived to a area where it wouldn't be able to see him. He could hear the animal moaning, "Oaouauao," as it ran right above where he was and fell in front of him, so he grabbed the spear out of the Bison and stabbed it again. It was a young calf Bison, still a great beast, but he realized this allowed him to be able to drag it back to his camp area. David gripped the animal and spent the rest of the day dragging it before having difficulties picking it up and putting the Bison in his box, so he used more of the tree limbs to make a basic ramp before finally being able to put the Bison in the box and put on the lid.

The next day as the sun came up, David jumped into the box with the Bison in order to cut it into large pieces that would be easier to cook. He took some extra sticks split at the top which he had taken from the trees, and put a leg on a long stick and placed it between the two split ones over the fire, and when a minute or had two passed, he would turn it so the other side of the leg could face the fire. David buried all the organs and ate the meat off the bone. He also removed the hooves before eating the meat that he enjoyed eating. Then he traveled with his clay bowl to collect water from the stream and returned back to his shelter with it full of water to drink in the morning.

Drinking some water upon waking up, David felt he could live out here for years. He laid down long sticks into the frame he had built for his shelter and cut out a place for a door. He quickly built one by stringing together many sticks with the grass, which he twisted together to form a rope that was stronger than plain blades of grass, and created a door. He also went to obtain more clay and relatively small rocks. With these items, he stacked up the rocks into a cylindrical structure and stuck clay in the crevices and used clay to cover the top with rocks. He left only a small hole. David started digging in the dirt to connect the cylinder to his shelter, and after that, he dug underneath the cylinder and held the flaming wood by the edges moving it into the cylinder. Going into his shelter, he also dug out a small hole around the outside of the tunnel. Although not efficient, he found there was enough heat coming into his shelter that it didn't matter.

When a week had passed, David woke up to see flies and bugs coming out of his box for the Bison, and as he pushed off the top, a swarm of flies came out at him. He was both disgusted and devastated at the loss of his meat. He found that smoking the meat wasn't the best idea for preserving the Bison, and there weren't many other options except to stuff himself whenever he caught a large animal, so he went hunting for something to eat. A rattlesnake came up to him and did what they do, rattling at him, so he backed away slowly, but held his spear firmly before he hurled it at the snake. Before it could react, it was dead, but had its mouth still moving, so he grabbed it from the back of the head holding the mouth closed. David held the snake over the hole in the top where the fire was and broke it apart in pieces before tearing off the scaly skin, finding it tasted like a chewy chicken.

He decided one day to go swimming in the ocean as he was finally getting settled into this routine of catching food and eating it immediately. He was having fun and getting exercise by swimming around, with waves often hitting up to his chin. David saw that he was going too far out into the ocean and was swimming back to shore when he felt the currents suck him under the water. He was trying to draw a breath but couldn't. The taste of salt coated his mouth. He knew from long ago to swim to the side of the direction the current is traveling. As he walked onto land, falling into the sand, he also recalled from history class that salt was a preservative used by countries many hundreds of years ago. He rushed back to his shelter, grabbing his clay bowl and ran back to fill it up with salty water. He let it sit in his shelter for twelve days, until the water dried and there was nothing but salt remaining. During that time he made a second clay bowl since he needed water that wasn't salty to drink.

David went to get more clay as it was possible that flies only got to his Bison meat because he used too much mud to fill the cracks with instead of clay. He lined the top lid, especially, with a whole lot of clay and pushed the lid down onto it so it would form to the lid before taking it off. Hunting for another Bison, he found another herd. In a few minutes he saw the smallest one protected by many of the adult Bison, so he followed the herd. He stayed a few hundred feet behind them hoping they might create a large enough hole in the circle around the small Bison where he could come within twenty feet and throw his spear. The Bison stepped through the grass, went over boulders, and came near to the forest before David finally got a small window of time. He ran up, stepping high to prevent his legs from making a lot of noise in the grass. His spear he threw with enormous strength as it went right into the animal. He dove into the grass thinking the Bison didn't have enough time to see him. The herd bolted away after seeing their dead offspring in the grass, so he picked himself up, to see vultures already eating his food and many more circling above. He held his spear and waved it around at the vultures saying, "Cah cah," scaring them into flying away. Although they were still circling, he dragged the beast several miles to his shelter, putting the ramp up and pushing it into the box before placing the lid on top and sitting on top to make sure the vultures didn't get in. When the vultures cleared out, David cut the beast up, roasting the pieces over the fire one by one, and after setting it back down, he salted the meat.

When a month and a half had passed, he felt tired and alone. He wanted someone around, or even a dog to talk to, but he had no way to get a dog out into the grasslands. He considered trying to capture the offspring of a Bison or wolf and making it his friend. One day he heard a sound of someone or something walking outside. David sneaked gently outside to see his container being ravaged by wolves. After they had finished, he followed them back to where the wolf pack lived; the wolves knew he was there, but there was another sound behind David. He turned around, but he could see nothing in the forest where the wolves lived. He turned his gaze back to the hole and walked slowly over to it; the pack of wolves watching him with curiosity as he crawled into the hole. He saw the mother for the pack staring at him with her pups around her. David laid on the other side of the hole waiting for the mother to get used to him. He inched closer to the mother, and proceeded to pet the wolf. The pups seemed old enough that he could take them and feed them regular meat, so he reached down to pick one up, but the mother didn't like him holding it. Waiting for another opportunity, he began to see that the wolves weren't going to let him take one. He heard more weird sounds that persisted while he traveled back to his shelter. He had a feeling of being watched, and at nightfall it sounded like there was someone running off in the distance into the forest, so David, on his bed made of grass, lay awake, and around midnight, from his perception there was a sound of a good number of people running. When he stepped outside his front door, no one was around, and his stomach felt like bugs were eating it from the inside. He went around and around the shelter, and with his eyes beginning to close, he forced himself to hold them open. His arms and legs felt weak, then there appeared a man a couple of hundred yards away. David stared at the man, trying to confirm his existence, but David was so afraid. With sweat running down his face, he ran away as fast as his legs could take him. He ran towards the city thinking he might lose him in the rolling hills–or in the city if that failed. David didn't feel tired anymore, but it brought even more terror when he tripped into a small cactus and got spines all in his clothes and was pricked by a few in his stomach. He could feel a headache arising. He never realized how far his legs could take him. After running so far, he glanced behind him and saw no one was still chasing him, so he settled down and started walking towards the city.

Chapter 7

The Event

When morning came, David was still walking and had reached the street into the city. *I'm gonna go back to my wife and kids. I mean, they probably didn't even notice I was gone, he said to himself.* He walked around the city a little bit, waiting for a better time of day to arrive home on the sidewalk, and tall apartment buildings gave him something to look at, although he got bored of it rather quickly, and there it was–his house with its driveway and windows. He ran to check if the door was unlocked, and when it wasn't, he pressed the doorbell a few times, and one of his children opened the door, looking at him for a moment before calling out,

"Dad!"

in excitement. David then walked up the stairs and into the bedroom to discover his wife wasn't there, so he went to check on the rest of his kids. Martha,

Jerry, and Boe were all well. He went to the restroom to look in the mirror to see how awful his teeth were. They were yellow and dirty and looked like they'd all fall out if he didn't brush his teeth immediately, so he scrubbed his teeth very gently with the toothbrush, thinking that brushing too hard might make them fall out. He heard his wife pull the red sedan into the driveway, so he went out the garage side door to see how she was and found that she was the same as when he had left. As he walked back into the living room, there was a newspaper on the marble counter at the edge of the kitchen. In the top right of the page, it stated,

> "Special REWARD, for anyone who gives information on someone who makes unusual faces."

David grabbed the newspaper, throwing it in the trash can next to himself, knowing what it meant by unusual faces. He made sure none of his children or his wife saw this act and took the garbage out to the usually green curbside trash can, although that didn't mean it would be picked up. What was confusing was how, many years ago, the idea of anyone remaining with other emotions was absurd.

When David walked back inside along the sidewalk up to the front door, he turned around, looking at the trash can and picturing the dark green of it in his head, the light green of the grass, and the blue of the sky. The color of the world was still there, only hidden from his sight, but David could at least attempt to bring that back within his mind.

Over the course of a few days, he checked the newspaper to see if the ad was still there, and it was, so he kept throwing the newspaper away.

"Why are there no newspapers?"

asked his wife, but David couldn't tell her the truth, because he knew the risk that could come with it. "Well, I thought it might be better if I read the news, and if you wanted the information from that newspaper you could come to me instead," said

David, and she nodded like she was hiding something, although it was hard to see through the face of someone who could only be happy. *Maybe she's read the ad in the newspaper before; I don't know*, he thought, *so I would really only be making myself more suspicious in her thoughts by telling this lie to her*. He watched as his wife took steps up the plain wood stairs, imagining the light brown of the banister and the steps, and she went inside shutting the door behind her.

David didn't want to run away again. He looked out the window as cars went by about once every fifteen seconds. He considered cars aren't common and that this was unusual, so he stepped up the stairs and opened the door to see his wife reading the newspaper that he threw away earlier in the morning.

"What are you doing?" questioned David.

"I'm figuring out where all the cars are going,"

she responded;

> "I might wanna go where they're going because since you left, the city has started having big events downtown."

He hadn't considered that his wife might want to do an event stated in the newspaper.

> "Okay, if you go, I'll go with you,"

he said, with a tone implying that if she didn't want him to go, he wouldn't, and he would be happy either way.

> "I want you to come,"

she replied, still sitting in a chair, reading the newspaper and glancing up at him every few seconds. David felt sweat beginning to collect on his forehead as he watched her eyes begin to move closer to where the ad would be, but it was still necessary to act calm.

> "Alright, let's go before it starts, wouldn't want to miss the event,"

he stated. She picked herself up out of the brown-stained chair and they walked down the stairs, through the garage side door and into a car that wasn't the red sedan David had owned for so many years. It was a gray SUV, and his wife tossed him the keys from inside the vehicle while he was standing with the door open. He was disappointed, not letting on that he wanted the sedan over this new SUV. He pressed the black button on the remote to open the garage door for his house, placed the key in the ignition, rotating it until the engine started, and sat there feeling the vibration of the car until he decided to back out of the garage. Luckily, there were still cars driving down the road every fifteen seconds or so, allowing for David to follow one of them. On the sidewalks, hundreds of people were going by foot to the event, which satisfied him that it must actually be fun as most people could easily entertain themselves at home. He watched the yellow-painted stoplight above the blue car in front of him, as it changed from green to yellow to red, and the car stopped as he slowed behind it to a stop. He turned to watch all the people go by, noticing his wife doing the same. David began traveling beside the people since he thought that would be easier than being behind another car.

He saw a theater in the distance with thousands of people in the audience and parked his car far in the back as hundreds of cars lined the sides of streets. Walking with his wife, he went through the gate at the front of the chain-linked fence, and his wife attempted to find some available seating as they walked around, finding only two available front row seats; they sat in them. It was hot, and a man with sweat on his forehead went up on the stage before the show they were going to show on the big screen. "I am proud to present to you a future where everyone will be truly the same. A world where you will be happier than ever, a place for you to live forever and ever," uttered the man, and the movie began as he walked off the stage. David swallowed, hoping this would only be something normal, but it was obvious it wouldn't be. His wife turned to him,

> "This is the update of the previous event; the speech was really only to help fill you and other first-timers in,"

she stated. The movie strangely began with deforestation that had trees replaced with metal towers before a quick cut to new homes coming off a factory line, to be put in place of the old homes. The music notes didn't flow from one to the next; it was like letting some cats run all over a piano with a violin orchestra playing next to it with violins that needed new strings. David glanced behind him; there were soldiers holding guns standing at the gate, blocking the exit. The screen showed a group of people and scientists putting people to sleep before cutting around their skull, pushing the top off and then yanking the people's brains out and throwing them in a contraption. Two people in the audience made a sound, "GGh," the soldiers walked over aiming their guns at them, and as they held up their hands the soldiers shot them in the heart. David saw that no one was watching this horror take place, so he slowly made a motion with his head, back to the movie screen. There was a dog with a brown fur color running in the grass playing happily, which was grabbed and given a piece of food that somehow altered its fur color to be gray, occurring within a month on a quick time-lapse video, and David realized it was the same color as the houses coming out of the factory and the metal towers replacing trees. Planes in the movie flew overhead and dropped gas on the many grasses covering the ground, and they all turned that same shade of gray. *This isn't some future to bring all the people happiness; this is a future meant to remove any color, any difference, any life in the world to a point that any person with a broader view would end themselves before they were even caught*, David realized as he thought about what was happening in the film. He wondered what was going to happen to the brains that had been yanked out of the people, but the man started walking back on stage,

"Alright, you all may go, and come back next month for the final portion of the film,"

he uttered as the people picked themselves up to walk out the gate and climbed into their cars. David followed, opening the car door for his wife before going around and entering himself as he saw the color of this SUV was that same gray color from the film and that many of the other cars around were the same make and model with the paint color.

"Well, I know what the previous film partially had in it now," David deduced.

He drove home, counting all the gray cars on the street. Far in the distance, he could see woodcutters cutting down all the trees and placing two metal towers on the farthest corners of homeowners' yards. David knew there was nothing he could do to stop them from removing the trees in his yard, so after pulling into the driveway and opening the car door, he went inside. He noticed their lamp and TV had been painted to be that gray color. The TV shows were presented in that color. He felt the vibration from the sound of the planes flying overhead changing the grass, and he could hear big trucks coming up the road with their new homes. He walked out the front door to see his trees had already been replaced, and the grass had also been altered. Deciding to go to bed early, he went upstairs before pulling down his lifeless blankets and jumping into his lifeless bed before covering himself up and lying awake. After some four hours of watching the clock, he fell to sleep. He did not dream as this was not a time to dream, but a time to mourn for what will become a lost existence. He awoke in the morning confused as he was not in the same bed, and he could only tell distinctions between things because of the shadows from the light they created. He moved his legs to the side of the bed and got up to look out the window where sunlight was coming through it.

"Looks great doesn't it!"

His wife seemed to proclaim for the world to hear,

"Yes, yes, it does,"

David was forced to reply, despite being disgusted at the sight of the ruined island.

"Come look outside, you ought to see this,"

his wife stated while grabbing him by the shirt and pulling him outside. Everything had become lifeless; the birds stood on top of the metal towers like statues, dogs in backyards appeared to be happily playing with their owners, but he knew they were really a blank piece of space occupied by atoms and molecules, useless for anything.

Homes were piled on top of each other forming apartment buildings, and as David realized this, he turned around to find that his home had four piled on top of each other. He knew it must be a home for him, his wife and one for every two children. Then he saw that the large trash bins hadn't been removed yet, so he could still more easily picture the color of those things, so he moved the recycling and garbage bins into his new home, with his wife becoming more watchful of what he was doing behind him. David closed the door, hoping his wife wouldn't immediately open the door behind him as he rolled the bins next to his couch and ran upstairs grabbing his bed sheet to cover them. He felt stress come like a man with a knife about to stab him. Presently, he thought about all that was happening and how the movie connected to it and then tried to piece together the first scene of the film. *The doctors are throwing the people's brains into some kind of contraption. What does that contraption do? It almost seems like their bodies don't matter anymore, but surely they're not just throwing those brains into that contraption and destroying them,* thought David, but the idea of their possible destruction made the hairs on his arm rise despite his not believing that's what was actually happening. His wife holding a new gray nineties flip phone, opened the door, and as the sunlight came in from behind, he saw the sky had even managed to become the tone of everything else without a single cloud existing.

David had made his decision to get off this island, to steal a boat, and to flee to wherever it will take him. His wife stood in the entrance of the house like a gatekeeper making sure he couldn't leave;

"I'm having people over for dinner,"

she stated, staring at him,

"Okay,"

he responded, while checking to make sure the window could be opened and had a latch to open it. He pulled up the window and climbed out the side on the bottom house with his wife watching. He ran and ran, reaching the edge of the island in an hour and then discovering there were no boats. Knowing there weren't any nearby islands to swim to, he turned around and stared at what his life would become if he stayed there. David stood quietly at the edge of the docks; *It couldn't be that bad*, he thought, *I mean, they're still at least similar to what people should be like*, and in that moment, three people came at him with masks on, put handcuffs on him, and carried him off.

Chapter 8

The Man Himself

Only David's shoes were touching the ground as the three people dragged him to an old police car and tossed him in the back. Two of them got in, and another one got in a gray SUV and drove behind them. The police car traveled very slowly, giving time to let David's fear rise and his gray clothes to become covered in sweat as his legs trembled with fear; he laid down flat on the backseat. The car was slowing down almost to a stop when he heard the engine make a loud noise. It roared into a wall that made David go flying against the front seats and fall on the floor below. Confused, he felt one person grab his shoulder sliding him out slowly as the car door opened. The three people still had their masks on so he couldn't see their faces as they dragged him over to a hospital bed, tying his arms and legs to the railing on the sides of the bed. David looked at what was around him, seeing needles for injections and many strange machines that went up to the ceiling as well as long metal rods. Watching as they went into the corner, he saw them whispering and strained trying to hear them, but he couldn't understand anything since the room was quite long.

They came over, grabbing metal rods from a table in the opposite corner. Beating David violently with their rods, they saw him stressed and in pain and almost beginning to cry a number of times. Then one of them grabbed a folder from a chair a few feet away as David wondered what he was writing about and how this event had to do with it. Seeing blood coming out of him and the dark red color of his shirt gave David a hint of pleasure even with the extreme pain that made him curl his body upward in agony. The three people walked out of an area he could see in his peripheral vision, but he did not want to suffer the pain of looking in their direction. There was a pair of hands hovering over his mouth holding a piece of food as they opened his mouth and shoved the food into his mouth. David knew the taste of this food: the despicable food kale, which he had always hated, and spewed it out of his mouth in disgust. He couldn't get that terrible taste out of his mouth and turned his face to once again see one of the group writing this event down in their folder before putting a good-tasting food in his mouth, which he recognized as potato chips, and the person continued writing. He felt something hit him on the head, and with all the other pain it didn't seem that bad, but it made him pass out in a period of seconds.

When David awoke, the lights weren't on and no one was around as his

"hello"

seemed to echo in his brain. In the room, there was nothing but pitch black darkness. He wondered if it was nighttime and they all went home, or if this was some other apparent test. He sat there thinking for many minutes, and the lights came on, but still nobody was around.

"Surely, I didn't get knocked out for hours?"

he pondered aloud.

"Hello,"

he uttered again more loudly. The lights cut out. He silently pulled on the ropes holding him to the bed, trying to make as little noise as possible. After a minute the lights came back on, and he stopped tugging. The door opened slowly as a person popped his hand in holding a gun. He pointed it at David without bringing the rest of his body in,

"HELP!, HELP!, someone,"

David yelled turning his head side to side lifting his body up and trying to avoid the gun, but it wasn't enough, and he kicked his legs as much as he could, shaking his arms as much as the ropes would allow him. The man's finger was on the trigger, and at the last moment, David closed his eyes, waiting for what appeared to be his destiny before reopening after a few seconds only to see the three people with the one writing the information down in his folder. The three men proceeded to open a compartment out of the wall that David would have never noticed and pulled out a TV. They tapped their fingers on the screen until finally pressing on a comedy called "Family Monkey." On the screen it stated,

"Last viewed five hundred twenty-six years ago".

The youngest child continuously got into trouble with his pet monkey and expressed himself more like people used to. David found it hilarious, but tried to hold in his laugh since the three people seemed to be able to tell and walked over and slapped him as he busted out laughing and couldn't stop himself. He had never seen something so funny because the modern TV shows were usually rather boring and similar to everything else. Once again, one of the three grabbed their folder which was shorter than the other folders and wrote something down.

"How did you come to be this way?" one of them asked.

"How?"

David didn't know how to respond or even if he should,

"Uhhh, I was born this way?"

he said, speaking with a questioning tone of confusion as he began to regret what he had said. He realized what their purpose was in taking him away, as it told them everything they needed to know. "Who told you I was like this?" he asked quickly so as to escape and be able to catch the person who gave him up to these people. One took off his mask, and David stared at him—looking at each part of his face—the short chin, the very large mouth, the cheek bones that came far out compared to the regular, everyday person. David knew him from somewhere, but he had no idea who he was until he uttered,

"Don't recognize me do you?"

"Clay?"

David questioned as the man began nodding his head.

"We're going to correct the issues you've been having,"

Clay responded in a robotic tone. Squinting at him, David knew Clay was here to remove his feelings and emotions, but hoping permanent happiness might cause stupidity,

"May I be released?"

David asked, but it was no use as the pleasure they got in fixing him was much stronger than any they'd get from releasing him.

"Ready for procedure,"

the other two people stated as one of them flipped a switch on the side of the wall, and engine noises sounded as they tied down David's head much tighter before grabbing a drill from under the bed. They switched the drill on and went around his whole skull as he screeched and tried to yank on the ropes holding him to the bed, but once again it was useless. One of them grabbed his brain as David screamed,

"NO!"

combined with incomprehensible vocal noise. He heard a bell go off on the large machine. They threw his brain into the contraption. All three watched as a different person walked out of the machine with only the name David. The region of his brain dealing with emotion was replaced. It now only allowed for happiness, but his person was not the same. David looked down at his old self; the two people took off their masks and pointed their index fingers at a wall where they pressed a button and flipped into a mirror. He saw that everything about him was a blank gray all over his skin. His eye color was gray, and he was bald—without eyebrows or anything on his face besides a mouth, eyes, and a nose. David absent-mindedly enjoyed it and saw that Clay was about to have the same procedure as they removed his original body from the bed and let Clay lay down. Then the two people spoke,

"You may go home if you wish;"

and that was all they told him, never speaking another word. David opened the metal door, and walked down a long narrow hallway painted white on the sides. He found pleasure in this gray world, no longer needing to picture the world as the color it should be in his mind. He read the sign saying "exit" that emitted a gray color. Pulling the door handle open with two glass windows and a steel frame, David looked down at his hand, noticing no more color in it and glanced at his clothes for a moment seeing the same thing. A problem arose, there was no way home. Every street had a sign that read nothing and had only a gray coating on it. Every building was the same, so he walked on the sidewalks most of the day, thinking of his past—what happened only a few minutes ago and the entirety of his life, trying to imagine what his life before must have been like, and there was true happiness in longing for what had become only memories. Then an SUV came out of its garage close to David, who didn't care to notice and was nearly completely crushed under its weight as he was rammed. He was lucky to get out perfectly fine, but he was in terrible pain that he found pleasing until after a few seconds. Then he thought he felt a slight stress rise up, but it quickly returned to happiness, and he continued on his way. His wife and children were standing outside their home as was everyone else, and he stated,

"I'm David,"

and she otherwise wouldn't have realized this,

"Would you like to come?"

she asked, and he didn't respond, but he followed her. Their children and everyone else got in their cars in near unison before driving off. After arriving at the event, a man quickly got up on the stage,

"We are nearing completion,"

is all he stated as he pointed to the same contraption at the back that had made David like this. Everyone was jumping up and down in excitement. Thinking harder, he remembered the stress he had felt from getting run over by a car and thought that pain might have caused it. In what would have appeared to be insanity to a normal person, he grabbed his arm and started biting himself. He hoped to bring about that feeling again. It was subtle, but he kept digging into his arm with his teeth, and in a wave of thought and feeling, he did feel like he had once felt, but there was no blood that ever came out. Before, when he could develop more complex thoughts and feelings, he would have bled, he wondered if that meant it was possible to cause other people to be like him— or at least he thought about trying.

David waited, wiggling in his seat, ducking low to prevent anyone from seeing him, with his wife and the other person in the seat next to him so focused on the man on stage that they would never notice what he was doing. He felt his skin, seemingly made out of clay, but he didn't know if it was some kind of non-hardening clay or a different material entirely. All the people got up, but David was still touching his skin when the man on the stage saw him. He pointed,

"That one first."

He told the soldiers, but the three original men were with the soldiers and came up to the front informing them,

"No he's ours;

we expected this to happen,

"we must take him back to a lab."

The man on stage agreed, so the people going to throw him in let go, and David was taken back to the lab in the back of a police car, handcuffed like before, but this time after they rushed, strapping him down to the bed, they made adjustments to the contraption. The three grabbed a different machine, and there was a sledge hammer lying against the wall opposite the door. They opened the door, and one went into a separate room in the hallway. David could see across the room where they took him in. The man came back after some minutes, dragging a different machine. All three pulled, and one took the sledge hammer. One who had a screwdriver, began screwing in the screws to connect the machine, and Clay took welding tools, using them to weld it to the whole machine. The man with the sledgehammer hit it once or twice to make sure the ball-shaped machine was attached to the contraption. David had experienced this before and wasn't about to let it occur again. He pulled the ropes and struggled to pull his body up while they were distracted since they forgot to totally tie him down. He chewed quietly with his teeth through one of the ropes on his hands, which allowed David to untie the other rope around his feet, being as careful as possible and every moment hoping they didn't turn around and stop him. He had the last rope almost completely untied when one of them turned and saw him. David hopped off as he pushed the bed, which was on wheels, in their way; they all dropped their stuff and ran to seize him. He dove over the table, placing his hands on the sledgehammer. He held it as a weapon,

"Get BACK!"

David told them, but they only slowed to walking pace, so he swung at Clay, who fell to the ground after being hit, and he practically threw the sledgehammer at the other two, hitting one. The third one he jumped on, trying to grab the sledgehammer off the ground, but it was too hard to pick up. David punched the person repeatedly and kicked him until blood could be seen through the person's clothes in big splotches. They all were dazed and at the time unable to fight back, so David got up off the floor, picked up the sledgehammer, and walked over to the contraption to begin trying to destroy it. He slammed it on the hole for brains and on the machine itself. It started smoking, but David kept going, eventually getting frustrated by how well-built the machine was considering that now it would only need minor repairs. He slammed it again and again until he got angry, hitting a spot that made the room fill with smoke in seconds.

The two people and Clay were no longer dazed, but the shock they had suffered from having some of their bones broken and being wounded, didn't go as David had expected. He thought it would bring out other emotions in them, and it did, but what they felt was not a real happiness, but a hatred for the pain he had inflicted upon them. This anger brought a willingness to kill that David saw on their faces as Clay held the welding torch in his hands. David knew the weapon in his own hand was no longer effective; nevertheless, he took the chance of swinging it at them, before quickly dropping it on the floor and grabbing the welding torch that Clay was holding with fire spewing out of it. Clay tried using his other hand to punch David, who grabbed his hand then let go and made a break for the door, but the two people grabbed hold of his shirt and smashed him against the contraption, causing a fire to start. to burn for a few moments on the edges before the contraption blew up. The whole room was on fire, with gray smoke filling the room so much that no one was visible, the largest area of the fire being where the contraption once was. David felt his chance to get away,

"IT won't OPEN! IT won't OPEN!"

one of them yelled, kicking and hitting the door with all his might. They were all beginning to value their own lives and losing a focus on David. Everyone heard a man on the outside, a liberation man, or so they hoped, but even with their yelling, he didn't care to open the door and thus liberating the four of them from their lives. Coughing and trying to figure out where they were in the room, the three of them saw their fate and laid down, giving into the pain. David, still wanting to live, tried to avoid the fire. He felt his legs burning and getting hard, and he could smell the other people burning to death, he heard them cry out in the unrecognizable language of agony, but he tripped into the fire, unable to see where he was, with his eyes, brain, tongue and memory of a life never to return; all melted away, leaving behind nothing but a shell of what once was a real person.

The clay hardened.

www.ingramcontent.com/pod-product-compliance
Lightning Source LLC
Chambersburg PA
CBHW060435130626
46555CB00005B/2368